THE SECRET DEAD

S. J. Parris is the pseudonym of the author and journalist Stephanie Merritt. It was as a student at Cambridge researching a paper on the period that Stephanie first became fascinated by the rich history of Tudor England and Renaissance Europe. Since then, her interest has grown and led her to create this series of historical thrillers featuring Giordano Bruno.

Stephanie has worked as a critic and feature writer for a variety of newspapers and magazines, as well as radio and television. She currently writes for the *Observer* and the *Guardian*, and lives in Surrey with her son.

www.sjparris.com

@thestephmerritt

By the same author

Heresy
Prophecy
Sacrilege
Treachery

The Secret Dead

S. J. PARRIS

HARPER

Harper
An imprint of HarperCollins*Publishers*
1 London Bridge Street
London SE1 9GF

www.harpercollins.co.uk

This paperback edition 2014

First published in Great Britain by
HarperCollins*Publishers* 2014

A catalogue record for this book is
available from the British Library

ISBN: 978-0-00-810209-8

Set in Sabon LT Std by Palimpsest Book Production Limited
Falkirk, Stirlingshire

Printed by CPI Group (UK) Ltd, Croydon CR0 4YY

MIX
Paper from
responsible sources
FSC
www.fsc.org
FSC™ C007454

FSC™ is a non-profit international organisation established to promote
the responsible management of the world's forests. Products carrying the
FSC label are independently certified to assure consumers that they come
from forests that are managed to meet the social, economic and
ecological needs of present and future generations,
and other controlled sources.

Find out more about HarperCollins and the environment at
www.harpercollins.co.uk/green

THE SECRET DEAD

I was eighteen years old and had just taken holy orders the summer Fra Gennaro found the girl. It was not the first time I had seen a naked woman. I had entered the Dominican order as a novice at fifteen, old enough by then to have tasted first love, the sweet warmth of a girl's pliant body in the shade of the olive trees above the village of Nola. A distant cousin, as it turned out; her family were livid. Perhaps that was why my father had been so ready to pay out for my education, though God knows he could ill afford it. Sending me away to the Dominicans in the city was cheaper than a scandal. We were given new names on taking our final vows, to symbolise the shedding of our old selves. I took the name Giordano, though most people just called me Bruno.

Naples in the summer of 1566 was an inferno of heat and noise, dust and crowds; a city of heart-stopping beauty and casual violence. Two hundred and fifty thousand souls seething inside ancient walls built to house one-tenth that number, the tenements growing higher and higher until their shadows almost shut out the sun because land was scarce, so much of it taken up by the vast gardens and courtyards of the palazzos and the religious houses. Tensions in the city

1

streets brewed and boiled like the forces of the great volcano that overshadowed them. Even walking from one side of a piazza to the other felt like fighting through the front line of an advancing army: elbows and fists, baskets, barrows and hot, angry bodies jostling and shoving, trampling or crushing one another. Horses and carts ploughed through the heaving marketplaces while the sun hammered down without pity and blazed back from walls of yellow tufa stone or the flashing blades of knives drawn in exchanges of rich inventive cursing. The Neapolitans discharged the tension by fighting or fucking, often at the same time. Soldiers of the Spanish viceroy patrolled the streets, though whether their presence imposed order or fuelled the general air of aggression depended on your view of our Spanish overlords. It was a city stinking of hypocrisy: kissing in public was illegal, but courtesans were permitted to walk the streets openly, looking for business even in the churches (especially in the churches). Blasphemy was also punishable by law, but beggars, vagrants and those without work were allowed to starve in the streets, their bodies rounded up each night on carts and thrown into a charnel-house outside the walls before they could spread contagion. Thieves, assassins and whores thrived and prospered there and, naturally, so did the Church.

In the midst of this simmering human soup stood the magnificent basilica of San Domenico Maggiore, where the faithful could worship the wooden crucifix that had once spoken aloud to St Thomas Aquinas. San Domenico was one of the wealthiest religious houses in the city; the local barons all sent their superfluous younger sons there as a bribe to God, and many of my brothers dressed and strutted like the young lords they still felt themselves to be, keen to preserve the distinction of degree despite their vows. The deprivations of religious life were interpreted here with considerable lassitude; it must have been well known to the prior and his officials that a number of the novices had copied keys to a side gate and often slipped out into the heat of the city streets at night, but I never saw anyone punished for it, provided they were back in time for Matins. Drinking, dicing, whoring – sins such as these were straightforward, easy to overlook in young noblemen with high spirits. It was sins of thought that the authorities could not countenance. In its favour, I should say that San Domenico prized other qualities than birth: it was famed as the intellectual heart of Naples, and a mere soldier's son like me might be admitted at the Order's expense if he showed enough promise as a scholar.

By early September, the city had grown heavy and slow, exhausted by the ferocity of the long summer's heat; people barely made the effort to curse as you pushed past them. There was a sense of apprehension, too; the previous autumn had brought a season of thick fogs off the sea carrying the contagion of fever and the epidemic had infected half the city. I had taken my final vows and been admitted to the Order in the spring, despite some misgivings on the part of the novice master, who confided to the prior that Fra Giordano Bruno had trouble submitting to authority and a taste for difficult questions. During my novitiate I had shown aptitude for my studies in the natural sciences, and the prior had set me to work for a while as assistant to Fra Gennaro, the brother infirmarian, in the belief that vigorous practical tasks – measuring, chopping and distilling remedies, helping to cultivate and harvest the plants used to make them, as well as tending to the ailments of those brothers confined to the infirmary – would occupy my mind and curb my wilfulness. In this he was mistaken; the more I learned about the natural world, its correspondences and hidden properties, the more my questions multiplied, for it seemed to me that our understanding of Creation, handed down from antiquity through the Scriptures and the Church Fathers, did not stand up to the most elementary scrutiny and observation. Fra Gennaro regarded my questions with forbearance and a hint of dry humour; for the most part he proved an attentive, if non-committal, audience while I formulated my doubts and theories aloud and only rarely did he reprimand me when I overstepped the bounds of what he judged a God-given hunger for knowledge. Few of the other friars would have shown such tolerance.

Fra Gennaro had studied medicine and anatomy at the famous medical school in Salerno; he had wished to become a doctor and eventually a professor, but some years earlier his family's fortunes had shifted for the worse, obliging him to leave the university and offer his skills in God's service. It was not the worst blow Fate could have dealt him – he was granted considerable freedom to further his medical knowledge in his new role, though I understood there was some dispute with the prior over the morality of using certain Arabic texts – but it was not the life he had aspired to and, though he never voiced this, I sensed in him a restlessness, a wistful longing for his old world. He was barely forty, but to me, at eighteen, he appeared to possess a wealth of knowledge and wisdom that I yearned towards – and not all of it sanctioned. In his heart he was a man of science, and a Dominican only incidentally, as I felt myself to be; perhaps this accounted for the instinctive affinity that quickly grew between us.

I was skulking through the darkened cloister one starless night in the first week of September, clouds sagging overhead like wet plaster and a warm, sickly wind sighing in off the bay, when I glimpsed him on the far side of the courtyard, his arms bundled full of linen. He was heading not to the infirmary but towards the gardens, in the direction of the outbuildings and storehouses at the furthest extremity of the compound, where the high enclosing wall backed on to a

4

busy thoroughfare. Something in his bearing – his unusual haste, perhaps, or the way he walked with his head down, leaning forward, as if into a gale – caught my attention. Though I risked punishment for being out of my cell at that hour, I called out to him, curious to know what he was about. If he heard me, he gave no sign of it, though I knew my voice must have carried. Instead he kept his eyes fixed on the ground ahead as he hurried through an archway and disappeared.

I hesitated in the shadows, hoping I would not run into the watch brothers. They made a tour of the cloisters shortly after Compline to confirm that everyone was tucked up in his cell and observing silence during the few hours of sleep, then retired somewhere more comfortable until their second circuit just before the bell chimed for Matins at two o'clock. If they knew of the nightly exodus through the side-gate in the garden wall, they were practised at looking the other way. But for a friar like me, with no family influence to consider and a growing reputation for disobedience, it would be a mistake to be caught. I could easily find myself a scapegoat for those they did not dare to discipline too harshly.

The air hung close, heavy with the scent of night blooms and a faint aroma of roasting meat from beyond the walls. Through the silence I caught the soft murmur of conversation drifting from the dormitory behind me, the occasional burst of laughter, the chink of Murano goblets. Fra Donato entertaining his fellow aristocrats, I supposed. The wealthier friars – those for whom the Church was a political career built on contacts and greased palms like any other – often held private suppers at night in their richly furnished rooms. As with the nocturnal excursions, the watch brothers remained tactfully deaf and blind to this.

Footsteps echoed behind me on the flagstones across the cloisters, over the low whisper of voices. There was no time to determine whether they were friend or foe; I slipped quickly along the corridor and through the archway where I had seen Fra Gennaro disappear. Here, behind the convent's grand courtyards, the grounds were laid out to gardens with an extensive grove of lemon trees. A path followed the line of the boundary wall, towards the side gate. If you continued past the gate to the far side of the trees, you reached a scattering of low buildings: grain houses, storerooms, the saddlery and stables. Beyond these lay a whitewashed dormitory of two storeys where the convent servants slept.

Without a moon, there was no hope of seeing which direction Fra Gennaro had taken, though if I strained my ears hard, I thought I could make out a distant rustling ahead among the lemon trees. The obvious explanation was that he must be attending to one of the servants who had fallen sick – but my curiosity was still piqued by his furtive manner and his pretence of not having heard my call.

Like every other novice, I had learned to navigate the path from the outer cloister to the gate in pitch-dark, feeling my way and calculating distance from the scents of the garden and the recognition of familiar landmarks under my feet and fingers: the twisted stalk of the vine that grew up the wall at the point where the lemon grove began; the slight downward incline as the path neared the gate. The footsteps persisted at my back, crunching on the hard earth. I moved off the path and into the shelter of the trees as two figures approached, fearing I had been discovered by the watch. But they paused a short distance away and I retreated further into the dark as I caught the wavering light of a taper hovering between them. Urgent whispers followed the scraping of metal against metal; I heard the creak of the gate and a gentle click as it closed again behind them. Novices or young friars heading out to the Cerriglio, the tavern two streets away, for a brief gulp of the city air before the Matins bell called them back to piety. I craned my neck and looked up through the leaves, wishing I could see the moon; I had no idea how late it was.

The gardens were unfamiliar to me beyond the side gate and I stumbled my way through the lemon trees, unsure if I was even moving in the right direction, my arms held up to protect my eyes from the scratching branches. After some while I emerged into open ground and could just make out the bulk of a row of buildings ahead. A horse whinnied softly out of the dark and I tensed; there were grooms who slept above the stables and would be woken by any disturbance. Holding my breath, I edged my way towards the storehouses and stood stupidly, looking around. Had Fra Gennaro come this way? Most likely he was already in the servants' dormitory, tending to some ordinary sprain or burn. How foolish I would look, lurking here in the shadows as if I were spying on him.

Minutes passed and I was debating whether to knock at the servants' quarters when I heard the muted creak of a door from one of the outbuildings behind me. A hooded figure slipped out and set down a pail at his feet. I heard the jangle of a key in a padlock, though it was clear he was trying to make as little noise as possible. A cone of light slid back and forth across the ground from the lantern in his hand. From his height I was certain it was the infirmarian, though I waited until he was almost upon me before stepping into his path.

'Fra Gennaro.'

'*Dio porco!*' He jumped back as if he had been assaulted, stifling his cry with his fingers as the pail clattered to the ground.

'I'm sorry – I didn't mean to startle you.' I moved closer, pulling back the hood of my cloak.

'Fra Giordano?' He peered at me through the darkness,

his breathing ragged in the still air. 'What in God's name are you doing here?'

'I wanted to offer my help.'

'With what?' Now that he had recovered from the shock, I noted the hard edge to his voice. He was not pleased to have been intercepted.

'Whatever you are doing. I saw you in the cloister and you seemed . . .' I searched for the right word '. . . burdened. I thought, perhaps—'

His mouth twitched to one side in a sharp noise of disapproval. 'You should not have been in the cloister. By rights I should report you to the prior.'

I lowered my eyes. We both knew it was an empty threat; I had given him better cause to report me before this and he had not done so. But he wanted me to know that he was angry.

'Forgive me, Brother,' I murmured. 'I was restless and needed a walk. When I saw you, I thought only to offer my assistance. I want every chance to learn. Is one of the servants ill? I could fetch and carry for you, if you let me observe the treatment.'

He did not reply immediately; only watched me with an unreadable expression, narrowed eyes glinting in the flame of the lantern. 'You wish to learn, huh?' He appeared to be weighing something up. After a moment, he stepped forward and gripped my upper arm so hard that I flinched away. His face loomed inches from mine, oddly intent; I could smell on his breath the ginger root he chewed to settle his stomach. 'There is much you might learn tonight, and I could use another pair of hands. But listen to me, Fra Giordano. I have been good to you, have I not?'

I nodded eagerly, unsure where this was tending.

'There are words you have spoken in my dispensary that anyone else would have reported instantly to the prior.

8

Words that would lead you straight before the Father Inquisitor. I have let them pass, because I recognise in you a spirit of enquiry that, while yet undisciplined, is born not of rebellion but of a true desire for knowledge.' He paused and sighed, passing the flat of his hand over his cropped hair. 'In that you remind me of myself. That is why I have not reported you for voicing opinions that to others would fall barely short of heresy.'

I bowed my head. 'And I am grateful for it. But—'

He held up a hand to pre-empt me and lowered his voice. 'Then we are both agreed you owe me a debt of confidence. You could assist me tonight, but you must first swear that you will never speak of what you see to anyone, inside or outside these walls.'

My gut tightened with excitement as my thoughts raced ahead, trying to imagine what kind of medical emergency would demand such a level of secrecy. I stared at him.

'I swear it. On my life.'

He peered into my face with that same fierce scrutiny, still holding my arm so tight that the next morning I would find a ring of violet bruises. Eventually it seemed he was satisfied. He gave a single curt nod and released his grip.

'Wait here, then. I must go to the dispensary to collect my instruments and heat some water. If anyone should come by, make sure they don't see you.'

'Why don't I come with you?' I offered. 'We could carry twice as much between us. Or, better still, they will surely have a fire in the servants' dormitory – could we not heat a pail of water there? It would make sense to be closer to the patient.'

He made an aggressive gesture for me to be quiet. 'The patient is not in there,' he said, dropping his voice until I had to strain forward to catch his words. 'If you are to work with me tonight, Bruno, there are two rules. You obey my every instruction, to the letter. And you ask no questions. Is that clear?'

I nodded. 'But why can't I come with you?'

'*Madonna santa!*' He threw up his hands and stooped to gather his pail. 'Because, as far as anyone knows, you are tucked up in your bed dreaming of saints and angels. Now do as I ask.'

He disappeared into the dark, until all I could see was the small spark of his lantern bobbing across the garden in the direction of the convent buildings. Silence fell around me, punctuated only by familiar night sounds: the snort and stamp of a sleeping horse, the drawn-out cry of an owl, the relentless, one-note song of the cicadas. Further off, a whoop, followed by a gale of raucous laughter from the streets beyond the wall. I pressed myself into the shadows of the outbuildings and waited. Where was this mysterious patient, then, if not in the servants' quarters? I glanced across to the door Fra Gennaro had locked behind him. In the storehouse? Why could he not be treated in the infirmary, like any other . . .

A sudden understanding flashed through me, flooding my veins with cold. This man must be an enemy of the state, someone it would not be politic for us to be seen helping. San Domenico had a reputation for fomenting resistance against the kingdom's Spanish rulers; it was well known that the more rebellious among the Neapolitan barons met regularly in the convent's great hall to discuss the form of that resistance, with the ready involvement of some eminent Dominicans. Perhaps this secret patient was a conspirator who had been wounded in the course of action against the Spanish. That would explain Fra Gennaro's insistence that I ask no questions. Pleased by my own reasoning, I bunched my hands into fists beneath my robe and slid down against the wall of the storehouse to squat on my heels, bouncing with anticipation.

I recited psalms and sonnets to measure the time; another twenty minutes passed before Gennaro returned, with a bundle tied over his shoulder and carrying the full pail of water, steam rising from the cracks in its lid. I leapt up and hurried to take it from him; he nodded and paused to check all around before fitting the key to the padlock. As soon as we were inside, he secured the door again behind us.

He held up the lantern and turned slowly to reveal only an unremarkable room with stone walls and a paved floor. Wooden crates lined one wall; barrels were stacked against the back. A sound of scurrying overhead made me jump; I looked up and a fine dust filtered through between the planks that had been laid over the roof beams to partition the eaves into a loft space. A ladder led up to a closed hatch.

'Only rats,' Gennaro muttered. 'Keep that light over here where I can see it.'

He gestured towards the furthest end of the room. At first I could not make out what he meant to show me, but as I drew closer with the lantern, I saw a wooden hatch set into the floor, the stones at the edges scraped clean where the crates concealing it had been moved away. The hatch was also held fast with a padlock. Gennaro selected another key from his belt, knelt and unfastened it. He paused with one hand on the iron ring and looked up at me, his eyes large and earnest in the flickering light.

'Your oath, Bruno, that whatever you witness here will remain sealed in your heart as long as you breathe.'

I could have taken offence that my oath was not good enough the first time; instead I was too impatient to see what lay beneath the door. Goosebumps prickled along my arms. I swore again, on my life and all I held sacred, my right hand pressed over my heart. Fra Gennaro studied me for a long moment, then lifted the hatch and led the way down a flight of stone steps into an underground chamber.

11

The air was cooler here, with a taint of damp. Though I could see little at first, on peering harder I made out an arched ceiling and walls lined with stone. No sound came from the dense shadows further in, none of the jagged breathing you would expect from an injured man. A cold dread touched me: suppose the patient had died while Gennaro was fetching his instruments and I was waiting uselessly outside? But the infirmarian showed no sign of panic. He closed the hatch and slid a bolt across so that we could not be disturbed. Next he unwrapped an oil lamp from the pack he had brought and lit it carefully from the lantern. In the brighter glow I saw that the chamber was dominated by a sturdy table draped with a thick shroud, under which was laid the unmistakable outline of a human figure.

A strange fear took hold of me, somewhere under my ribs, constricting my breath. Gennaro removed his cloak and hung it on the back of the door, indicating that I should do the same. In its place he shrugged on a rough hessian smock, such as the servants wear, and over this a wide leather apron. Then he rolled up his sleeves, dipped his hands into the steaming water and rubbed them clean before opening the bag he had brought with him. In the lamplight I caught the flash of silver blades. The last item he extracted was a large hourglass, which he set upright on a box beside the table to allow the sand to settle. When he had assembled all the equipment to his satisfaction, he took one corner of the shroud in his hand and glanced at me.

'Ready?'

I tried to swallow, but my throat had dried. I managed a nod, and he pulled back the sheet covering the body.

In the stillness I heard myself gasp aloud, though I had the presence of mind not to cry out. Stretched out on the table was the body of a young woman, about my own age, unmoving as a marble tomb. Her flesh was so unblemished

12

that it seemed at first she might be merely sleeping; indeed, I dared to hope as much for the space of a heartbeat, until I looked more closely and saw in her face the unmistakable contortions of strangulation. It was clear, despite the bulging eyes, the protruding tongue and the discolouration of the face, that she must have been unusually beautiful, not very long ago. Her skin was pale and smooth, her dark hair flowed around her shoulders and her waist was small and neat, her hips narrow and her breasts full. Ripe bruises like shadow fingers formed a ring around her white throat.

'By my reckoning,' Gennaro said, turning over the hour-glass, now brusque and businesslike, 'we have about two and a half hours until Matins. There is no time to waste.'

So saying, he took a broad-bladed knife and slit the girl's shift lengthways in one swift movement, from hem to neck, leaving the fabric to fall away either side. I tried to avert my eyes from the dark thatch of hair on her pubic mound, but it was difficult; I had not seen a woman's body in three years. If Gennaro noticed my confusion and the colour rising to my cheeks, he was discreet enough not to mention it.

'Who is she?' I whispered, fixing my gaze on her feet. The soles were bare and dirty.

'Beggar. Homeless. Come, hold that lantern closer.' His reply came just a fraction too quick.

'But – how does she come to be here?' I blurted, forgetting my earlier promise.

'She was found in the street by one of the night patrols and brought to me. They thought they might be in time to save her. Alas, they arrived too late.'

He could see that I did not believe this version of events. I was not convinced that he did either. No Spanish soldier in the city would trouble himself to help a vagrant girl. They were more likely to be the ones who had abused and killed her. At least he had the grace to look away as he said it.

'But she has clearly met with a violent death, and quite recently—'

He laid the back of his fingers on the girl's neck, his expression speculative. 'An hour or so, I would say.'

'Then surely we should report it?'

'Fra Giordano, I thought we had agreed no questions?'

I bit my lip. He paused and straightened, his hand hovering over a selection of knives. I could not miss the impatience in his face, though his voice was softer. 'Listen. You told me you have read the work of Vesalius.'

'I have, but—'

'And how did Vesalius come by his knowledge of the human body? Where did he find his raw materials?'

'He stole corpses from the gallows at night.' I felt as if an invisible hand were squeezing my own throat.

'Exactly. And you know he also robbed graves? In the pursuit of understanding, it is sometimes necessary to interpret the law in one's own way.'

'But this girl has been murdered! He may not have got far – someone might have seen something—'

'That is not our concern, Brother.' The sharpness in his tone took me by surprise. He sighed. 'In the medical schools of Europe, professors of anatomy are allocated the bodies of felons for public dissection under the law – as many as four a year in some places.' His jaw tightened. 'I will never be a professor of anatomy now. God in His wisdom saw fit to call me to His service in another way. But that does not mean my desire to learn is any the less.' His tone suggested a degree of scepticism about the divine wisdom in this instance. He planted both hands flat on the table and leaned across the girl to nail me with a fierce stare. 'Listen to me, Fra Giordano. I see in you the makings of a man of science. I mean it. For such as us, pushing the boundaries of what is known, shining the light of true learning into the dark corners of Creation

– there can be no higher good. I know you agree.' He jabbed a forefinger into the air between us. 'And do not let anyone make you afraid of God's judgement. All of Nature is a great book in which the Creator has written the secrets of the universe. Would He have given us the gifts of reason and enquiry if He did not wish us to read that book?'

In the soft light, his face was avid as a boy's. I hesitated. Fra Eugenio, my novice master, had taken great pains to impress upon his flock of intellectually ambitious youths that the first and greatest sin of our forefather Adam was the desire for forbidden knowledge. He held firmly to the view that the Almighty intended much of His creation to remain beyond our meagre human understanding. I was of Fra Gennaro's mind, but I was still afraid.

'You mean to anatomise her.' My voice emerged as a croak. This time I did not frame it as a question.

He picked up a long knife and studied the tip of its blade. 'You know as well as I that this city is overrun with indigents.' He gestured with the knife towards the figure on the table. 'She was a street girl, a whore. No one will mourn her, poor creature. If she were not lying here now, she would be on a cart full of corpses heading for Fontanelle. At least this way some good will come of her sad existence before she ends up there. In life she gave her body up to rogues and lechers. In death, she will give it up to the service of anatomy.' He fixed me with a long look, tilting his head to one side as he pressed the knife's point into the pad of his finger. 'You are not obliged to stay, if your conscience advises you otherwise. But think of the opportunity. You are the only one here I would trust to assist me.'

I looked at him. How could I resist such flattery? Even so, in my gut I was deeply troubled by his proposition. In the first place, I did not believe his story about how he had come by the body. There could be no doubt that the girl had been

15

murdered, barely an hour ago, and I feared that in disposing of her corpse – to say nothing of illegally dissecting it – we would be implicated in her death. More than this, though, it was the brutality of what he was proposing that disturbed me. I had read Vesalius's work on anatomy and understood the value of practical experimentation. But this girl had already suffered violence at the hands of a man; whatever she may have been in life, our cutting and probing in the name of scientific enquiry seemed like a further violation. I did not voice any of this. Instead, I said:

'Does the prior know?'

He allowed a long pause. His gaze slid back to the girl on the table.

'The prior has, on occasion, given me permission to examine corpses where it is clear that there would be some greater benefit in doing so. When old Fra Teofilo died last year in Holy Week – you recall? – I was permitted to cut him open in order to study the tumour in his gut. And what could be more beneficial than furthering our knowledge of the female form? You cannot know how rare it is to find such an ideal specimen.'

The gleam in his eyes as he said this verged on lascivious, though not for the girl, or at least, not in the usual way. His desire was all for her interior, for the secrets she might yield up to his knife. From his studied evasion of my question, I took it that the answer was no. He tapped the hourglass with a fingernail. The sand was already piling into a small hill in the lower half.

'Time will not wait for us, Bruno. Go or stay, but make your mind up now.'

'I will stay,' I said, sounding steadier than I felt.

'Good.' Relief rippled over his face. 'And if you think you are going to faint or vomit, give me plenty of warning. We will have enough to clear up without that.'

He dipped a cloth in the hot water and wiped it almost tenderly around the girl's chest, along the declivities of her clavicle, the sharp ridges of her collarbones and into the valley between her breasts. 'Note the fullness of the breasts,' he observed, as if he were addressing students in an anatomy theatre, as he marked the place of the first incision in a Y-shape across each side of her breastbone, 'and the enlargement of the areola. If I am right in my speculation, we may find something of unparalleled interest here.'

I concentrated on holding the lantern steady over the table. As if I could have failed to notice the girl's full breasts or large, dark nipples. Perhaps he had forgotten what it was to be eighteen. In his eyes she was simply a specimen, material for experimentation. To me she was too recently living, breathing, warm, with a head full of thoughts and dreams, for me to regard her as anything other than a young woman. I did not dare touch her skin; I almost believed it would still hold some pulse of life. Nor could I look at her face; the terror in those wild, staring eyes was too vivid. I had heard it said that, when a person was murdered, the image of the killer was fixed in their death stare. I did not mention this to Fra Gennaro; I did not want him to laugh at me or take me for a village simpleton.

Any unbidden lustful thoughts shrivelled in an instant as he pushed the blade into her flesh. He made two careful incisions along the breastbone and joined them in a vertical cut that ran the length of her torso to her pubic mound. The sound of the knife tearing through meat was unspeakable, the smell more so. I recoiled, shocked, at the amount of blood that pooled out. Gennaro calmly placed containers under the table at strategic points, and I saw that, like a butcher's block, the surface had channels cut into it that diverted the blood into tidy streams of run-off that could be collected underneath. He folded back the skin on each side of the chest cavity, exposing the white bones of the ribcage. I clamped my teeth together, fighting the rising tide of bile churning in my stomach, reminding myself that I was a man of science. A wave of cold washed over my head and a sudden sunburst exploded in my vision; the cone of light from the lantern slid queasily up and down the wall. Gennaro stopped to look at me.

'You've gone green.' He didn't sound greatly sympathetic. 'Hang the lantern on that hook above me and sit down with your head between your knees. We can do without you passing out on her.'

I did as I was told. I sank to the cold floor at the far end of the room with my back pressed against the wall, clasped my hands behind my head and buried my face in shame. The terrible slicing noises continued, the determined sawing through resistant muscle and tendon, the sucking sound of organs being displaced. I closed my eyes and bent the whole force of my will towards maintaining consciousness and keeping my supper down. I could not tell how much sand had slipped through the glass by the time I felt able to stand again, but when I opened my eyes and levered myself to my feet, Fra Gennaro was bending over the girl's exposed abdomen with an ardent expression. His eyes flickered upwards to me.

'You're back with us, are you? Come and look at this.' He prodded with the tip of his knife. He was indicating a swollen organ about the size of a small grapefruit, mottled crimson. 'The greatest anatomy theatres in Europe would pay dearly to get their hands on this. It is an opportunity granted to very few anatomists. Providence has smiled on us tonight. Do you know what it is?'

I considered replying that Providence had been less kind to the girl, but I merely shook my head.

'This is the womb, Bruno. The cradle of life. Locus of the

18

mystery of generation. The source, it is believed, of all female irrationality.' He reached in with bloody fingers and tugged, frowning. 'Hippocrates said it had the power to detach itself and wander about the body, but I do not see how that could occur. This one seems firmly attached to the birth canal.'

He parted the girl's legs and quite perfunctorily inserted two fingers into her vagina, pushing up until he could feel the pressure with his other hand. 'Interesting,' he murmured. 'It seems to me that Vesalius's drawing of the female reproductive organs is seriously flawed . . .

'And now,' he continued, lifting the girl's womb towards him as if he were a street conjuror about to reveal his greatest trick, 'watch closely and learn. For if my guess is correct, you are about to witness a secret that some of the most renowned anatomists in Leiden or Paris have yet to see in the flesh.'

He took a smaller knife and made a precise cut in the outer skin. As it ruptured, a clear, viscous fluid spilled out over his hands along with the blood. Gennaro peeled back the skin and extracted from within the womb a tiny homunculus, no bigger than the span of my hand, but already recognisably human. He laid it in his palm, his eyes bright with wonder.

'Is it alive?' I breathed.

'Not now. You see this?' He nudged with the knifepoint to the twisted white tube that still connected its abdomen with the interior of the womb. 'It can't live without the mother. This is very early gestation, see? A matter of weeks, I would say. But note how you can already make out the fingers and toes.'

The creature had the translucent sheen of an amphibious animal, its half-formed limbs and curved spine so delicate as to seem insubstantial. Perhaps it was his casual use of the word 'mother', but I felt a sudden terrible emptiness, a

19

hollowing-out, as if it were my insides that had been torn away. This homunculus would have grown into a child, if the girl's life had not been cut short by those hands around her throat. I wished fervently that I had never followed Gennaro. I began to fear I lacked the detachment to make a man of science.

Fra Gennaro carefully excised the womb and the tiny foetus, severed the cord that bound them, and placed each into a large glass jar he had brought in his bag. 'But where does it *come* from?' he muttered, as he sealed the jars.

'From the man's seed.' I was unsure if he was addressing the question to me, nor even if my answer was correct, but I needed the distraction.

'Ah, but does it?' He looked at me, seemingly pleased. His cheek was streaked with blood where he had touched it. 'Opinion is divided. There are those who say the womb is merely the field of Nature in which the seed is planted, and others who think there is some additional element contributed by the woman, without which the seed cannot germinate. What think you?'

'I imagine these elements are so small as to be invisible. So that we can only study the effects and must work backwards to infer the cause.'

He nodded and wiped his hands on his apron. 'It may be that we will never unravel the mystery of conception. But that does not mean we should not try, eh? I shall study this further.' He patted the sealed lid of the jar containing the foetus. I had to look away.

From somewhere beyond the thick stone walls of our underground mortuary came the distant tolling of a bell. My head snapped round and I met Fra Gennaro's eye. Neither of us had noticed how long ago the sand had run through the hourglass. I glanced down at myself; my habit was daubed with the girl's blood and God knows what else.

20

Gennaro pulled his apron over his head. 'I need fresh water and new candles,' he said, decisive. 'I will tell the prior you are taken sick and unable to attend Matins. Close the hatch and draw the bolt after me and do not open the door to anyone until I return. I will give three sharp knocks.'

Before I could object, he was gone. I climbed the stairs and slid the bolt across, shutting myself in with the girl. She lay splayed out like a carcass at the butcher's, yellow fat and livid red organs bright against her pale skin. I drew closer to the table, torn between fascination and fear. In Gennaro's absence, I felt emboldened to test the theory of the killer's image by looking into her eyes, but all I saw was naked terror and my own reflection. It seemed apt, in a twisted way; I could not escape the feeling that we were as guilty of her destruction as the man whose fingers were imprinted around her slender neck. I backed away, chilled by an irrational fear that she might suddenly turn her head and fix me with those eyes. I tried to intone the psalms but the words stuck in my throat. Instead, I turned over the hourglass and watched the sand drain through in a fine dust. The minutes that passed until I heard Gennaro's knock were some of the longest of my life.

'We need to dispose of her before first light,' he said, brisk again. 'I will need your help.'

'How?'

'We must take her to Fontanelle.'

'But the city gates will be locked until dawn.'

He slid me a sidelong look. 'They can be opened.'

He crossed to the far side of the room and unlocked a wooden door in the back wall. I had been so intent on the girl I had not noticed it before. A breath of cleaner air filtered through and I saw that the door opened on to an underground passageway.

'Part of the network of tunnels and cisterns belonging to

the old Roman aqueduct,' Gennaro explained. 'It links to another tunnel beyond the boundary wall and comes out on the other side of Via Toledo. Here – help me with this.'

From the passageway Gennaro dragged a cheap wooden casket into the room. I grabbed the other end and helped him position it alongside the table. When he opened the lid, I saw that it was lined in oilcloth, and the inside was already bloodstained. He drew out a coarsely woven cloak from beneath the lining, such as the poorest wear in winter. It smelled thickly of decay.

'There is one thing I need to do before we transport her,' he said, draping the cloak over the casket and turning to face me with a stern look. 'You may prefer not to watch this, Bruno. I have to skin her.' He turned back to the table and selected a knife with a thin, cruel blade.

Again, that strange lurch in my gut, as if I had missed a stair. 'Why?'

'So that she cannot be recognised. People may be looking for her.'

'You said there was no one to mourn her.' I heard the accusation in my voice.

'Mourn her, no. But if she was a whore in this neighbourhood, her face will be known. The remains we send to Fontanelle must not be identifiable.'

'It's barbaric.'

He made an impatient noise with his tongue. 'Perhaps. But it is also prudent. What we have done here tonight would be hard to explain to the city authorities. I think you see that.'

I bowed my head. 'Then no one will ever be brought to justice for her murder.'

He laid down his knife and looked at me with an air of incomprehension. 'You think they would otherwise? A street whore?' He shook his head. 'I admire your fervour for justice on behalf of the weak. It is, after all, part of our Christian duty,' he added, as if he had only just remembered. 'But it is not our concern here, Bruno. There will be no justice for her in this life. Pray God grant her mercy, and retribution to those who wronged her in the next.'

With this, he grasped a hank of her lush hair and sliced it through cleanly at the roots, as I turned my face away.

All through the long journey to the Fontanelle cavern, he did not say a word to me, except once, to ask if I carried a dagger. When I said yes, he gave a dry laugh. 'Of course you do. This is Naples. Even novice nuns carry a blade beneath their habits.' I wondered if he was afraid the girl's killer might still be lurking nearby. I tried to shut out the thought that Gennaro knew more about the murderer than he was letting on.

We took turns pushing the cart with the makeshift coffin, the two of us wearing old servants' cloaks with the hoods pulled up close around our faces, despite the warm night, so that we would not be recognised as friars. I could not tell if Gennaro was angry with me for questioning him, or for my squeamishness, or if he was just tired. Reducing the girl to hunks of bloodied meat had not been an easy task. The human body is tougher than it looks; limbs need to be wrenched from sockets, bones sawed through, joints separated with a hammer. Gennaro must have been exhausted, but he did it all alone, while I sat with my back against the wall and my head in my hands, trying to shut out the sounds. What he packed into that box, wrapped carefully in oilcloth to stop the blood dripping through the wood, was no longer human. I stole glances at the casket as he led us through the twisting back streets in the dark, his face dogged and clenched in the light of my lantern.

A couple of times we turned a corner to find a group of

young men staggering home from the taverns, arms slung around one another's shoulders, half-empty bottles dangling from their hands. Each time I braced myself, my hand twitching to my knife in case they should decide to have some sport with us, but they looked at the cart and steered a wide berth around it, their raucous songs faltering away to nothing as they eyed the box. No one wants to be reminded of death in the midst of their revels. I suppose they took us for those men who clear the beggars off the streets. At the Porto San Gennaro I saw the glint in the darkness of coins changing hands as the infirmarian exchanged a few words with the guards, who seemed unsurprised to see him. One of them nodded, before unlocking a small side gate and gesturing us through.

The road began to slope steeply upwards into the Capodimonte hillside. With the incline and the stony track the cart became harder to move, as if it were resisting its destination; we had to put our backs into the work and within minutes I was soaked with sweat beneath my cloak. I had no idea how far it was to Fontanelle – it was not a place I had ever thought to visit – and I did not like to risk Gennaro's anger by asking him. I knew only that it was a great cavern up in the hills, left behind by the excavation of tufa for building. In the early years of the century, the Spanish authorities had begun clearing the city's churchyards to make room for more bodies, and the old remains had been taken to the Fontanelle cave. Since then it had become a dumping ground for the city's outcast dead: those who could not afford or had been denied burial in consecrated ground. Lepers. Sodomites. Suicides. The *lazzaroni* – the nameless poor who died in the streets. Plague victims were thrown in, whenever there was an outbreak. Fontanelle had become a great charnel-house of the unwanted; people said you could smell it from the north gate if the wind was in the wrong direction.

I caught the stench as the incline grew steeper and the track widened out into a plateau; rotting flesh and stale smoke, the kind of bitter ash that hung in the air and worked its way into your nose and mouth as you breathed. A man lurched forward out of the shadows to greet us; again, the chink and flash of money from somewhere inside Fra Gennaro's cloak. A small brazier burned by the entrance to the cavern. In its orange glow, I saw that the man's face was badly deformed, though his body looked strong; his brow bulged low over one side like an ape's and he had been born with a cleft palate. Perhaps this was the only place he could find work. At least the dead would not throw stones at him in the street, or shout insults. He and Gennaro spoke in low voices; I had the sense that they too were familiar with one another. I watched as the man took the cart and wheeled it towards the mouth of the cave, a maw of deeper shadows that swallowed him until he disappeared from view.

I turned to see Gennaro studying me.

'Are you all right?' he said.

Beneath my robe, my legs were trembling as if with cold. I told myself it was the climb. I gestured towards the cave.

'What if he tells someone?'

'He won't.'

'How do you know? Surely you can't see a body in that state and not ask questions?'

'Part of his job is knowing not to ask questions.' Gennaro squinted into the darkness and pulled his cloak tighter. 'Besides, he won't bite the hand that feeds him.'

I did not immediately grasp his meaning, until I thought of the coins chinking quietly into the man's hand, their familiarity. Of course: this would not be the first time Gennaro had brought a dismembered body here for disposal under cover of darkness, no explanations required. I wondered how many other illegal anatomisations he had carried out in that little mortuary under the storehouse, with its convenient tunnel for ferrying bodies out unseen.

The man returned with the cart and the empty box.

'I'll let you know if I find anything suitable,' he muttered, darting a wary glance at me. Gennaro gave him a curt nod and turned again towards the road.

A pale glimmer of dawn light showed along the eastern horizon as we walked back down the track, the city a dark stain below us.

'Does he sell you bodies?' I asked bluntly.

Gennaro looked sideways at me. 'Remember your oath, Brother.'

We walked the rest of the way in silence. Under the cloak I could feel stiff patches on my robe where the girl's blood had dried. I wondered how I would explain that to the servant who came to take my laundry.

'I prescribe a hot bath for this fever that has kept you from tonight's services, Bruno,' Gennaro said, as if he had heard my thoughts. 'I will instruct the servants to fill the tub in the infirmary. Clean yourself well. I will see to your clothes.'

'Will you write about this?' I asked him, as we approached the gate.

He smiled, for the first time since we had set out. 'Of course. This is one of the most important anatomisations I have ever performed. To study a child *in utero* is a rare piece of luck, as I told you.'

Not for the child, I thought. 'But you cannot publish your account, surely?'

'True. At least, not in Naples, and not under my own name. Eventually, however, who knows . . .' His voice tailed off and his eyes grew distant. Perhaps he was dreaming of a book full of his experiments and discoveries.

'But in the meantime – are you not afraid someone will find your notes?'

He smiled again, like a child holding a secret. 'I keep them very safe. And I trust you, as I said.'

I forced myself to return his smile, though he meant that I was now as deeply implicated as he was. In ways I could not yet fully comprehend, I felt irreversibly altered by what we had done that night. Despite scrubbing myself with scalding water and a bristle brush until my skin grew raw, I could not erase the smell of blood, nor the memory of the girl's wild death stare. Fra Gennaro made me up a bed in the infirmary, so that I was excused the office of Lauds on account of my supposed fever, but I could not rest. If I closed my eyes I saw her walking towards me with her hands outstretched, pleading, before she reached up and tore the skin from her own face until it hung in tatters from the bloodied pulp beneath.

The following night, I barely waited until the sun had set before slipping out of the side gate and through the alleys to the Cerriglio. I needed company, drink, the easy conversation of my friends. Pushing open the door, I was assaulted by its familiar heat and noise, the animated shouting of a dozen different arguments, its odour of charred pig fat and young red wine and sweat. In the back, someone was strumming a lute and singing a love song; his friends were filling in bawdy lyrics, howling with laughter. I stood still for a moment on the threshold, allowing the tavern's chaos to crash over me, pulling me back to the world I knew. I had not been able to eat all day, and now the smell of hot bread and meat tickled my throat, filling my mouth with salt and liquid.

At least half the Cerriglio's customers were young friars from San Domenico and their companions. Gaudy women moved among the tables, stroking a forearm or sliding a finger under someone's chin as they passed, gauging the response. One caught my gaze as I stood there and I blinked quickly away; when I looked at their painted faces, all I could see was the bone and gristle beneath the skin.

I scanned the room, looking for my friend Paolo. Laughter blasted across from the large table in the centre, where Fra Donato was holding court, as usual. He glanced up and saw me standing alone; his eyes narrowed and he leaned across and muttered something to Fra Agostino beside him, whose lip twisted into a sneer. Neither of them troubled to hide the fact that they were talking about me. I had barely spoken to Fra Donato, but I knew his reputation. His father was one of those Neapolitan barons who had managed to cling on to his land and titles under the Spanish, which led people to speculate about what he offered them in return. But he was a valuable benefactor to San Domenico, and his son was regarded as a prior in the making, despite the boy's obvious distaste for the privations of religious life. Fra Donato was tall and unusually handsome, with the blond looks of a northerner; it was said he was a bastard and his mother a courtesan from Venice, or Milan, or even, in some versions, France or England. Whatever the truth, his father indulged him generously and he, Donato, had certainly learned the trick of buying influence. He was a few years older than me; I had not expected to attract his attention, but recently I had been aware of his scrutiny in services and at chapter meetings. I guessed I had been pointed out to him as a potential troublemaker, and that this had piqued his interest. Now, though, hot with the fear that people could smell the girl's blood on my skin, I could not help but interpret any suspicious glances as proof that someone had seen me last night and knew my dreadful secret. I felt the colour rising in my face as Donato and his friend continued to whisper, their eyes still fixed lazily on me.

'Bruno!'

I whipped around at the sound of my name and saw Paolo at a corner table with a couple of his cousins, a jug of wine between them. He raised a cup and I hurried over, grateful to be rescued.

'I thought you had a fever?' He poured me a drink and handed it over.

'It broke in the night. I'm fine now.'

He grinned. 'Well you look fucking awful. Are you sure you should be out of bed?'

I gulped down the wine, feeling its warmth curl through my limbs. I was about to make some light-hearted comment to fend off any further questioning, when I was prevented by a commotion from behind us. Voices raised in anger; glass shattering, the crash of furniture hitting the floor. I turned, and I swear that, just for an instant, my heart stopped beating.

The dead girl stood in the centre of the tavern, in front of Donato's table. She had knocked over a chair, it seemed, and dashed the glass from his hand. A blood-red puddle spread across the table and dripped slowly on to the floor. She was shaking with rage, her right hand extended, pointing at him. The hubbub of music and conversation died away in anticipation; people always enjoyed a good fight at the Cerriglio.

It was her; there was no question about it. The same glossy fall of black hair, the marble skin, the delicate features and wide-spaced eyes as unspoilt as they would have been in life. The same slender throat, unmarked now. But she had knocked over the chair; how could that be, if she was a spirit? I held myself rigid with fear, my hand so tight around the cup I feared it would crack, though I could not will myself to move. I did not believe in spirits of the dead and yet, buried deep, I had not shaken off the childhood memories of my grandmother's tales, of revenants and unhallowed souls returning to be revenged on the living.

The girl balled her fists on her hips and cast a defiant glance around the room. I froze as her eyes swept over me, but there was no flicker of recognition. If she had come for vengeance, surely I would be her first target? But she turned her blistering gaze once more to Donato, threw her head back and spat in his face.

A cheer went up from the onlookers, all except Donato's comrades. He wiped his cheek with a sleeve, but his movements were those of a sleepwalker. He was staring at the girl with a mixture of horror and disbelief.

'Where is she?'

'Who?'

'You know who!' The girl quivered with rage.

Donato rose to his feet and attempted to recover some dignity. 'You have me confused with someone, *puttana*. I do not think I know you. Unless I was more drunk than I remember last night.'

This won him a smattering of laughter from the crowd. The girl tossed her hair and her eyes flashed.

'Oh, you know me, sir. And I know who you are.'

'So do most of your sex in Naples.' More laughter.

'Have you killed her?' Her voice was clear and strong; she made sure everyone could hear.

Donato paused, as if catching his breath. The mood in the room shifted; you could feel it like the charge in the air before a storm. He leaned across the table.

'I have no idea what you are talking about. But if you accuse me of anything in public again, I will see you before the magistrates for slander. Now get out.' He allowed a pause for effect, before adding, cold and deliberate: *'Jewess.'*

The word hung between them like the smoke that follows a shot. The girl stared at him as if she had been struck. A sharp intake of breath whistled through the crowd, followed by a startled cry; in a heartbeat, the girl was up on the table, silver flashing in her hand. Fra Agostino pushed Donato out of her reach, a lamp rolled to the floor and smashed, someone screamed, and then the doorkeeper they called L'Orso Maggiore (for obvious reasons) shouldered his way into the mêlée and wrenched the girl's right arm behind her back, sending her knife clattering to the ground. She carried on yelling and spitting curses as he dragged her off the table and towards the threshold, as easily as a bear would pick up a rabbit.

'Where is her locket?' she roared, at the door. She repeated the same question, louder, as L'Orso hurled her out into the street. You could still hear her cries, even when the door slammed after her. Gradually, the hubbub of conversation resumed until it drowned her out.

'Donato really should learn to take more care where he puts it,' remarked Paolo, shaking his head as he reached for the wine. 'He'll ruin his father with paternity suits one of these days.'

'Paternity suits?' I turned to look at him.

'Some neighbourhood girl accused him a couple of years ago, threatened to make a fuss. His father had to pay the family off. Sounds like he's at it again.' He gestured towards the door, then glanced at me. His brow creased and he laid a hand on my arm. '*Madonna porca* – are you sure you're all right, Bruno? You're white as a corpse.'

'I need some air,' I said, pushing the table away.

Donato was bleeding from a surface cut on his forearm where the girl had made contact before she was hauled off. His hangers-on fussed around him while the rest of the tavern stared as they exchanged animated whispers. Signora Rosaria, who owned the Cerriglio, was berating L'Orso for not stopping the assault sooner; the crowd pressed in for a better view of the drama. No one had noticed the girl's knife lying on the tiles under a neighbouring table. I ducked down and slipped it into my sleeve on the way to the door.

There was no sign of her in the street. I walked a little way along between the tall houses, towards the corner of the next alley, thinking I had lost her, when I caught the sound of muffled sobs. She was crouched in a doorway, her right arm cradled against her chest. After the initial shock of seeing her in the tavern, my frantic thoughts of vengeful spirits had given way to a more logical explanation, but I was still afraid to speak to her.

Alerted by my footsteps, her head snapped up and she sprang back, her hands held out as if to ward me off. The street was sunk in darkness, except for the dim glow from a high window opposite and the streaks of moonlight between clouds. The girl's face was hidden in shadow.

'I think this is yours.' I offered the knife to her, hilt first. Her eyes flicked to it and back to me; for a long time she didn't move, but I stayed still and eventually she began to approach, wary as a wild dog, until she was close enough to snatch it. She levelled it at me; I raised my empty hands to show that I was now unarmed.

'Who are you looking for?'

'What is it to you?' She bared her teeth. 'I know you are one of them. I have seen you here before.'

'*Them?*'

'Dominicans.' She spat on the ground at my feet. 'God's dogs.'

'You know Latin?' I said, surprised. It was an old nickname for the Order, a pun on *Domini canes*, the Hounds of the Lord, but I had not expected to hear it from a woman, especially one who was clearly not high-born.

'Yes. You think a woman cannot read? Hypocrites.' I thought she was going to spit at me again but she restrained herself. 'Look at yourselves. You take vows of poverty and chastity, and yet there you are, night after night, dicing and whoring like soldiers. And they made you the city's

Inquisitors, the ones who decide whether others are practising their religion to the letter, and if they should die for it.' She let out a short, bitter laugh. 'God would spit you out of His mouth.' She was lit up by her fury, illuminated from within, every inch of her taut and quivering. She wanted only the slightest provocation to stick that knife in me, I was sure of it.

'That man you attacked,' I said, keeping my voice steady. 'What has he done?'

Her lip curled; she reminded me again of a dog that knows it is cornered and is readying itself to fight. 'I suppose he is your friend? Did he ask you to make me repeat it, so he could accuse me of slander?'

'He is no friend of mine. I only wanted to help you.'

'Why?' The word shot back, quicker than a blow. She took a step closer, holding the knife out as if I had threatened her.

I shrugged. 'Because we are not all hypocrites.'

Her eyes narrowed; she did not believe me. She was right not to, I reminded myself: I was the biggest hypocrite of all.

'My sister,' she said, in a subdued voice, just as I had assumed she was about to walk away.

'Your twin?' The words were spoken before I could stop them; she stared at me, her mouth open.

'Why do you say that? Do you know her?'

'No . . . I . . .' I blushed in confusion. 'I don't know why I thought that.'

'Yes, my twin,' she said, lowering the knife, as if the fight had gone out of her. 'That friar –' she nodded past me in the direction of the tavern – 'he saw me in the street one day and followed me to our shop.'

'What shop?'

'My father keeps a shop on Strada dell'Anticaglia, off Seggio di Nilo. He is a master goldsmith. That man started coming into the shop to court me. I refused him. I would not be the mistress of a monk, for all his money. I have no respect for your kind.'

'So you have said.'

A muscle tightened in her jaw. 'He would not take no for an answer. Then one day he came into the shop when my father and I were out and found my sister instead.'

'He took her for you?'

'I don't think he cared either way. But Anna was always flattered by the attention of men.'

Anna. I thought of a flayed leg thrown into a makeshift coffin like an animal carcass, stripped to the crimson muscle and white bone. She had had a name. Her name had been Anna.

In this girl's face I saw again the lineaments of her dead twin. A whore, Fra Gennaro had said. Was that his lie, or Donato's? My skin felt cold, despite the warm wind.

'And she went with him?'

'She started sneaking out after dark to meet him. She never told me where she was going, but I followed her one night. She made me swear to secrecy. She knew it would break our father's heart.'

'He would have been angry?'

'He would have killed her.' As soon as she had spoken the words, her hand flew to her mouth. I felt something lurch in the hollow under my ribs, some pulse of hope. The girl's father found out, he killed her in a fit of rage, perhaps by accident; so Fra Gennaro's story could be true. Even as the idea formed, I knew it was absurd.

'I meant only . . .' she faltered, through her fingers. 'He has never lifted a hand to either of us in our lives. But the shame would have destroyed him.'

'Back there, you accused the friar of killing her,' I said. 'Was that a figure of speech too?'

34

She drew her hand slowly away from her face and took a deep breath. It escaped jaggedly, like a sob. 'My sister is missing. She went to him last night and she has not returned. I know she has come to harm.'

'Perhaps she has run away.' As I spoke, I felt as if there was a ball of sawdust lodged in my throat. My voice sounded strange to me.

The girl shook her head. 'She would never have done that. In any case, I followed her last night too. I was afraid for her.'

The ball in my throat threatened to choke me. I feared she could hear the thudding of my heart in the silence.

'To the Cerriglio?'

'No. She went to San Domenico and waited for him by the gate. I saw her go in and she never came out.'

A warm breath of air lifted my hair from my forehead and cooled the sweat on my face. Beneath my feet the ground felt queasy, uncertain, as if I were standing on a floating jetty instead of a city street.

'You must have missed her,' I said, but the words barely made a sound.

'I waited until first light. I could not have our father wake and find us both gone. I would swear she did not leave. Unless there is another entrance. But then, why did she not come home?'

I felt my palms grow slick with sweat at her mention of another entrance. I should have let her go then, but I had to be sure of how much she knew. 'Why do you think he meant her harm, if they were . . . involved?'

'Because she—' Her face darkened and she turned away. 'Her situation had changed. She was going to ask him for something he could not give.'

'Money?'

The slap came out of nowhere; she moved so fast I barely

35

had time to register that she had raised her hand. Rubbing my burning cheek, I reflected that at least she had not used the hand that held the knife. I stretched my jaw to assess the damage, but she was already stalking away around the corner.

'Wait!' I ran after her, into another, narrower alley. She turned, eyes blazing out of the darkness.

'My sister was no whore, whatever he says.' She paused, and I saw that she was fighting back tears. 'She believed herself in love with him.' She swiped at her eyes with her knuckles. 'What is any of this to you? Why are you following me?'

'If your sister was inside the walls of San Domenico last night, someone must know something.' I was surprised at how level my voice sounded, how carefully I controlled my expression. Only a few months since my vows, and already I had acquired the Dominican talent for dissembling. Though it was a skill that was to serve me well in later years, in that moment I despised myself to the core. 'What is your name?'

'Maria.' Most of the women in this city are called Maria, but she hesitated just long enough for me to understand that she was lying too. 'Yours?'

'Bruno.'

'Well then, Bruno. You know where I can be found. But I will not hold my breath – I know your kind always stick together. Whatever has happened to my sister, he will not face justice for it. Not in this city. A family like mine, against a man of his name?'

I wondered what she meant by that, and recalled the quiet, deliberate cruelty of Donato's last insult to her. 'Why did he call you – that?' I asked.

Her expression closed up immediately. 'I expect it was the worst abuse he could think of.'

We looked at one another in silence for a moment, her eyes daring me to question further.

36

'What about the locket?'

Her mouth dropped open, the fury in her eyes displaced by fear.

'What do you know of that?'

'Nothing. Only that I heard you accuse Fra Donato of taking it.'

Her hand strayed to her throat; an involuntary gesture, I supposed, as she thought of her sister wearing the locket. I could think only of the bruises around the dead girl's neck.

'If he has taken it . . .' She faltered. I sensed that she was weighing up how much to say. 'It has little value for its own sake. But it belonged to our mother. I *must* have it back.' The note of desperation in her voice told me she was withholding something. She feared that locket falling into the wrong hands – but why?

I stood foolishly staring at her, wishing I could offer some consolation, cursing the weight of what I knew – the truth she would spend the rest of her life raking over and not knowing. Or so I had to hope.

'You know where to find me if you hear anything,' she said again, with a shrug. I was about to reply when, silent as a cat, she turned and disappeared into the blackness between the buildings.

I crashed through the door of the infirmary, careless of the hour, careless of the noise I made. Fra Gennaro was bent over the bed of old Fra Francesco by the light of a candle, applying a poultice to his sunken chest to ease the fluid on his lungs. Gennaro started at the sound of the door, but as soon as he realised it was me, his expression told me he had been expecting this.

I glanced along the length of the infirmary, my ribs heaving with the effort of running through the back streets. Four beds in the row were occupied by elderly friars who wheezed and grunted in concert; they might have been asleep, but they might also have been quite capable of hearing and understanding. It was all I could do not to blurt out my accusations; Gennaro saw the urgency in my face and gestured me towards the dispensary, whispering words of reassurance to Fra Francesco as he stood to follow me.

'She was not a whore, was she?'

He closed the door behind us and set his candle down on the dispensary bench, signalling for me to lower my voice.

'I told you only what was told to me,' he said. His tone was clipped and cold, tight with suppressed anger.

'And you chose not to question it.'

He was across to me in one stride, his hand clamping my arm, face inches from mine.

'As I recall, Fra Giordano, you also swore an oath to ask no questions. Who have you been talking to?'

'I didn't have to talk to anyone.' I dropped my voice to an urgent whisper. 'Tonight her mirror image walked into the Cerriglio and accused one of our brothers of murdering her twin.'

He stared at me, his grip slackening.

'She was never found in the street by soldiers. She died inside these walls, didn't she? That's why you would not speculate on who killed her. Because you already knew.'

He breathed out hard through his nose, his eyes fixed on me for a long pause, as if I were a favourite son who had disappointed him. Eventually he let go of me and rubbed his hands quickly over his face like an animal washing.

'Where would we be, you and I, if we were not here?' he said, looking up.

I blinked at him, unsure whether it was a rhetorical question. He raised his brow and I realised he wanted an answer. 'If you had not come to San Domenico, Fra Giordano, what would you have done with your life?'

38

'I would have tried to obtain a place at the royal university,' I mumbled.

'Would you? The son of a mercenary soldier? With whose money?'

I looked at my feet.

'My father was well born, but he died desperately in debt to a Genoan banker,' he continued. 'If I had not come to San Domenico, I would most likely have had to beg for a position as a tutor to idle rich boys. And you, Bruno – I doubt you would be now be the most promising young theologian in Naples, whatever you claim.'

I said nothing, because I knew he was right.

'We are alike, you and I.' His voice softened. 'Neither one of us, in our hearts, desired the constraints of a religious life. But it was the only door open to us. You acknowledge that, surely?'

I gave the briefest nod.

'Then you also understand that it is not the likes of us who keep San Domenico afloat. Our scholarship may contribute to its reputation, but it is men like Fra Donato, with his name and his father's vast endowments, who ensure its continued prestige and wealth. We are the beneficiaries, and we would do well to remember that.'

'So he must be protected, at any cost. Whatever he does. This man who might be prior one day.' I turned away in disgust.

'What else would you do? Call in the magistrates? Destroy the whole convent and college with a scandal, for the sake of one foolish girl?' He rubbed the flat of his hand across his cropped hair. 'I admire your sense of justice, Bruno, I have already told you that. But you are young. If you want to make your way in this city, you must learn to be a realist.'

I wanted to tell him that folly did not deserve death, that

39

her name was Anna, and she did have people to mourn her. I wanted to protest that a rich and well-connected young man was not entitled to snuff out a life merely because it had become inconvenient to him. But I could say nothing without revealing that I had been asking questions. My gaze shifted away to the rows of glass bottles and earthenware jars ranged along the shelves. The dispensary always smelled clean, of freshly crushed herbs and the boiling water with lemon juice that he used to scrub down his table and instruments, a contrast to the stale fug of sickness and old bodies that hung over the infirmary. Somewhere in here a tiny, half-formed child was suspended in alcohol, in a jar. Donato's child.

'Suppose someone knew she came here last night, and comes in search of her?'

Gennaro's brow lowered; he fixed me with such a penetrating stare that I almost feared he could see my deception.

'Why should you imagine that?'

'Her clothes did not look like those of a whore. Perhaps,' I added, as if I had just thought of it, 'when you first found her, she was wearing some jewellery that might identify her? If we knew who she was, we might be better prepared to defend ourselves against any accusations.'

He sighed, as if the conversation were keeping him from something pressing. 'The girl came here alone last night. Donato took her into the lemon grove – they argued, and he grabbed her by the neck to frighten her into silence, he said, for he feared she threatened to make a scene and rouse the whole convent. She resisted, and he held her harder than he intended. Her death was an accident.'

'You know that is a lie,' I said, quietly. 'He meant to silence her all right. She must have told him she was with child.'

He brought his hand down hard on the table. 'The business is done now, Bruno. There is no evidence that she was ever here.'

40

'Did he ask you to help dispose of her?' My voice sounded small and uncertain in the thick silence of the dispensary. 'Did he know what you were going to do?' With every question, I was unpicking the fine thread of trust that existed between me and Gennaro, but I could not stop myself. I wanted the truth. He had brought me into that room with her corpse last night; I felt it was the least he owed me. A sigh rattled through him and he leaned back against the workbench as if he needed support.

'Donato came to me in a blind panic last night, shaking all over. He told me what I just told you – that this young woman had come to the gate, demanding to talk to him. He had taken her into the lemon grove, away from prying eyes, and they had argued, he grabbed her by the throat, she fell to the ground. He claimed he thought she had merely passed out – he wanted me to go with him to see if I could revive her.'

I made a scornful noise. 'He must have known she was dead.'

'Well, he was in no doubt as soon as I saw her. He was on the verge of hysteria – he was begging for my help. She could not be discovered inside the walls, obviously. Our only option was to move the body as far from San Domenico as possible before anyone noticed her missing.'

'But you decided to cut her up first.'

His eyes slid coldly over me. 'It was not my first intention – though I knew it would greatly lessen any chance of the convent being implicated if her body was made unrecognisable. It was only when he mentioned that they had argued over her threat of a paternity suit . . .' He trailed off, tracing one finger along the grain of the table's surface.

'You saw an opportunity that some of the leading anatomists in Europe would sell their own souls for.' I thought of the embryo, silent and transparent in its jar.

That cold sheen in his eyes intensified; he pointed a finger towards me. 'Do not be so quick to judge, Giordano Bruno. The advance of knowledge demands a certain ruthlessness. It is a quality I do not doubt you possess yourself, though you have not yet fully discovered it. I told Donato if he would help me move the body to the storeroom, I would see to it that she was not found anywhere near San Domenico. He was greatly relieved, I think, to have shifted the problem on to someone else's shoulders.'

I said nothing, but I could not look at him. Gennaro folded his arms across his chest. When he spoke again, his voice was kinder.

'The only accusations that can harm us now are coming from your own conscience, which you must learn to silence, or you will put us all in jeopardy. She is no longer your business. Do not give me cause to repent of my belief in you, Bruno.'

I lifted my head and met his gaze. In his stern expression I saw anger tempered by a fatherly concern. I had thought I was being tested, to see how much I was prepared to risk in the pursuit of knowledge. Now I felt deceived; this had not been about the advance of science at all. What we had done was all in the service of protecting a murderer and the name of San Domenico. A murderer who might one day be the head of the most powerful religious house in Naples. I wished bitterly that I had never thought to follow Fra Gennaro last night. Not that my ignorance would have changed anything, but I would have been spared the weight of this guilt.

From beyond the window, the chapel bell struck a long, low note.

'You had better get yourself to Matins,' he said. He reached a jar down from a cabinet to his right, unstoppered it and pulled out one of the ginger and honey balls he kept for throat complaints in winter. 'Here. Take one of these – I can smell the tavern on your breath. And Bruno . . .' he called, softly, as I opened the door. I turned, expectant.

'Remember your oath.'

I nodded. But I also remembered my promise to Maria.

At first light, shortly after Lauds, I crept out of my cell again and crossed the gardens to the lemon grove. I scoured the ground, fancying I could see here or there in the parched earth and scrubby grass some sign of a struggle, but there was nothing conclusive. Nothing to say that the girl had ever set foot here. I searched among the trees for almost half an hour, in vain. Gennaro had deftly ignored my question about jewellery; perhaps he had disposed of the girl's locket in case it should identify her, or perhaps hc had never seen it. A necklace chain could easily be broken if you were fighting off a pair of strong hands around your throat.

The bells had just rung for Prime when the sun slipped out from behind its veil of cloud and I caught a metallic glint at the foot of a twisted trunk. I knelt and fished out from among the dried stalks a chain with a gold pendant. An oval, about the size of a large olive, faced with exquisite filigree work and a finely wrought figure of the crucified Christ on the front. I wondered if the girl's father had made it. The chapel bell sounded its sonorous note again and I glanced up to see Fra Donato crossing the grove towards me in rapid strides. With his bright hair lit by the early morning sun, he looked like a painting of the newly risen Christ, if Christ had ever glared at someone as if he wanted to burn them alive with his eyes. I barely had time to slip the locket inside my habit and stand, hands folded demurely into my sleeves, to greet him.

'Brother. *Pax vobiscum.*'

'What are you doing here, Fra Giordano? Shouldn't you

43

be at prayer?' He had no authority over me, except that afforded by seniority and birth, though he addressed me as if he were the prior himself. His cold blue gaze swept over the lemon trees and seemed to comprehend the scene in a glance. He had come in search of the locket too, I was certain.

'I *am* praying, Brother. I felt moved to speak to God here among the trees, where I can meditate on the wonders of Creation.'

'Perhaps you should have joined the Franciscans.' He left a pause. 'Do you know, they say you are the most promising scholar San Domenico has seen in a generation.' I shrugged. 'They do not say so in my hearing.'

'Well, of course not. They would not want to provoke you to the sin of pride.' He tilted his head to one side. There was an intensity in the way he held my eye that made me understand why a woman might fall under his spell. That and the remarkably fine features, the bones that looked as if they had emerged from a sculptor's vision of an archangel. 'I hear you have a prodigious memory too.'

I made a non-committal movement with my head. 'It serves.'

'That is a great gift,' he said, as if he were granting me a rare concession. 'But even with your powers of memory, Brother, certain things are best forgotten. That scene in the tavern, for instance. A woman who believes I slighted her sister or some such thing. Women do not take well to feeling scorned, you know. It can quite turn their wits. They will say terrible things in their fury.'

'I barely recall it,' I said.

He gave me a sliver of a smile. 'Good. It's just that I thought you went out after her.'

'No, Brother,' I said, composing my expression into one of perfect sincerity. 'I had been unwell. I went out because I felt sick and needed air.'

He was watching me carefully, I knew. 'Well, I hope your health is improved,' he said, in a lighter tone. 'We had better not be late for Prime. They also say you show a particular aptitude for your Hebrew studies,' he added, as I turned towards the path. I stopped, remembering his insult to Maria. Was he insinuating something? 'A surprising aptitude,' he repeated. 'Almost a *natural* fluency, apparently. Is there Hebrew blood in your family, Fra Giordano?'

'No.' I regarded him with a steady eye. 'My family has lived in Nola for generations. You may make any enquiries you wish.'

'Oh, I have,' he said, with a pleasant smile. 'Your father is a soldier, is he not? And a soldier for hire at that – not even an officer.' He sounded regretful. 'Still – with the right patronage, a young man with your rare abilities might achieve great things in the Dominican order. You were fortunate to be admitted to San Domenico. Without your place here, I fear your exceptional talents would go to waste.' His eyes skated over me from head to foot as he spoke, as if he were trying to detect whether I was concealing anything.

'I do consider myself fortunate, Brother.' I lowered my gaze to demonstrate deference.

'You might prove it by showing a little less disregard for the rules,' he said. I jerked my head up and stared at him, indignant. He laughed and stretched his arm out to pull down a branch of the tree above us. 'No doubt you think me a hypocrite for saying so. But here one has to earn the right to a degree of flexibility. You are very cocksure for a friar who has barely taken his vows. Not my words, Brother, but those of others who have noted your tendency to pick and choose when to honour the vow of obedience. And I do not believe you have the learning to challenge the authority of Holy Scripture in the way you do. I offer this as a friendly warning. But you should be aware that they are keeping a close eye on you.' He snapped off the twig in his hands and stood there, twirling it between his fingers.

I walked away. I did not know if there was any truth in his words, but the warning itself was not to be ignored. Donato was certainly watching me, and he wanted to be sure I knew he could break my future as easily as that branch. When I reached the far side of the gardens I glanced back to see him under the trees, searching the ground and kicking at the grass with the toe of his calf-leather shoes.

As soon as I was alone in my cell for silent prayer, I opened the locket. The clasp sprung with a satisfying click, to reveal a miniature portrait of a dark-haired woman. It was cheaply rendered; the paint blurred in places so that it was hard to make out her features, though I assumed it must be the girls' mother. I turned the locket over in my hand, perplexed as to why Maria should have been so afraid of losing it. I pictured again the flash of panic in her eyes, the desperate catch in her voice. Perhaps it was more valuable than she admitted, or it was all the sisters had to remember their mother. But I could see that the back of the golden oval was deep and rounded, though the portrait it contained was flat. It looked as if it had been designed to contain something more substantial than a picture. Something concealed behind it, perhaps. Such things were used for smuggling secret communications, I had heard. With this sudden under-standing, my skin prickled into goosebumps. Of course a master goldsmith would know how to work a hidden compartment into a pendant like this. The question was how to find the opening without damaging the mechanism. I worked at the clasp with the tip of my knife with no success, before trying the same trick with the hinge on the other side. I nicked my fingertips so many times the surface and the blade grew slippery with blood, until at last I heard a catch give and the back of the locket opened smoothly. I licked the blood from my fingers, wiped them on my habit and drew out a folded square of parchment.

The writing on it was tiny and densely packed, though neat and precise as if it had been written with a quill as fine as a needle. But my heart was hammering as fiercely as the moment I first saw the girl's body, for the characters written there were Hebrew. I mouthed the first words – *Shema Yisrael* – and realised I was holding a text more dangerous than anything I had read in my life. This was a copy of the Shema, from the Jewish prayer service. Anyone found to possess this would be immediately summoned before the Inquisition, with little hope of a pardon. No wonder Maria was so terrified of it falling into the wrong hands.

Officially there were no Jews left in Naples. They had been expelled in 1541, though a few had chosen to convert and stay. Maria's father must be one such *convertito*, if he was permitted to trade here as a Neapolitan. I had heard that their houses were raided occasionally to ensure that they had truly renounced the faith, but it was rumoured that some had managed to cling on to their traditions in secret. I recalled the deliberate cruelty of Donato's insult to Maria; the way she had flinched as if he had struck her. The insinuations he had made to me – that he could taint me with the same slur if he wished. What did he know of Maria's family history? If the girl Anna had believed herself in love with him, how much might she have confided? To hide the Shema in the locket suggested that, however tentatively, she had chosen to hold on to her identity. Surely she would not have given up such a dangerous secret to a man who belonged among the city's Inquisitors, no matter how strongly she felt for him?

I folded the parchment and replaced it in the locket

with trembling fingers. As I closed the secret compartment, I saw that a drop of blood from my finger had stained the edge of the prayer crimson. I could not think what to do. In my heart I knew I had no choice but to return the locket to Maria; I understood its value now, not least as a memory of her dead mother and her sister. But to return it was as good as confirming that I knew something about the girl's fate, and the bloodstain on the parchment would surely fuel their fears; they would take it for hers. I could not keep it. Fra Gennaro would no doubt see it as more evidence to be erased, so I could not ask for his help. I hid it again inside my undershirt and prayed earnestly for guidance.

Despite Fra Donato's warning that I was being watched, I decided to miss my theology class after the midday meal, asking Paolo to say I was still feverish, and slipped out into the tired heat of the city. With my hood pulled up around my face, I cut along Via Tribunali in the direction of the Duomo. Strada dell'Anticaglia stood steeped in shadow from the high buildings closing in on both sides. Lines hung with washing dripped on me from above as I passed under the ancient arches of the Roman theatre that spanned the street, seeming to hold up the houses. I walked quickly, my head down, scanning the doorways and barred windows for the sign of a goldsmith's. After walking the length of the street, I returned to the only shop that seemed likely, though it had no marker outside, and peered through the small window. Inside, a man stood canted over a workbench with two lamps lit beside him; though it was the brightest hour of the day, the sun would never penetrate to the interior of this little shop in its canyon of a street. He held a thick lens to one eye to magnify his vision as he worked with a delicate, tweezer-like tool. I could see only the top of his head: greying curly hair and the beginnings of a bald patch the size of a communion wafer.

A bell chimed as I entered the shop. The man looked up with a smile that froze on his lips as he registered my habit. He lowered the lens and straightened his back with an air of resignation.

'Have you come to search my home again, Brother? It is barely two months since they were last here.' He sounded as if the prospect made him weary rather than angry. 'We are true Catholics, as we have been for twenty-five years.'

Twenty-five years. He could not be much over fifty; that would mean he had been little more than my age when he had been asked to choose between his history and his home.

'No, sir,' I said, quickly, appalled to have caused him alarm. 'I hoped I might speak to your daughter. Maria.'

His face hardened. 'Neither of my daughters is home at present.' As if to betray him, the ceiling creaked with the footsteps of someone walking in the room above. My eyes flickered upwards; his remained fixed calmly on me. In the light of the oil lamp I saw that his face was drawn, his dark eyes ringed with shadow. One of his daughters had not come home for two days; he must already fear the worst. I wondered if Maria had confided in him about her sister's lover, the pregnancy, or where she had last seen Anna. I doubted it; she had said the knowledge of her sister's affair would break their father's heart. She would want to protect him from the truth.

There was nothing more I could do. Inside my habit, the locket pressed against my ribs in its hidden pocket, but to hand it over would be as good as announcing that his daughter was dead, and implicating myself.

'No matter. Perhaps one day I will come back and buy a gift for my mother.' I turned to leave.

'I should be honoured, sir.' He gave me a slight bow and a

half-smile; despite his understandable dislike of Dominicans, he knew that he needed our continued favour.

I felt a pang of empathy; though I could not imagine the constant threat that hung over this man and his family, no matter how sincerely devout he tried to appear, I already knew what it meant to harbour secret beliefs in your heart, beliefs that could lead you into the flames before the Inquisitors' signatures had even dried on your trial papers. The more I studied, the less convinced I was that the Catholic Church or her Pope were the sole custodians of divine wisdom. I could not tell if it was fear or arrogance that led the Holy Office to ban books that might open a man's mind to the teachings of the Jews, the Arabs, the Protestants or the ancients, but I felt increasingly sure that God, whatever form He took, had not created us to kill and torture one another over the name we give Him. Tolerance and curiosity: a dangerous combination for a young Dominican at a time when the Church was growing less and less tolerant. I nursed my doubts like a secret passion, relishing the shiver of fear they brought. I wanted to tell the goldsmith we had more in common than he realised. Instead I returned his bow and left the shop, the bright chime of the bell ringing behind me.

A few paces down the street I stopped under the Roman arch and tried to think what I might do with the locket. I could wait until the shop was closed and try to push it under the door or through a window, in the hope that Maria would find it. But someone else might see it first, and think to look inside its secret compartment. I could not risk that. I could walk down to the harbour and throw it into the sea, where it could not incriminate anyone. Though I hated the idea of destroying something so precious, this seemed the only safe course, for all of us. I had almost reached the end of the street when I heard quick footsteps behind me, and turned to see Maria running barefoot through the dust.

'I went to Fontanelle,' she announced, pinning me with her frank gaze. I stopped absolutely still. I dared not even breathe for fear of what my face might betray. Every muscle in my body was held rigid. She let out a long, shuddering sigh and her shoulders slumped. 'Nothing. No bodies of young women found in the past two days.'

'Then perhaps she has run away after all,' I managed to say, hating myself for it, though relief had made me light-headed and my legs weak. I leaned one hand on the wall for support.

Maria shook her head. 'I will never believe that. I thought you might have come to bring me some news?'

I hesitated, then reached inside my habit and brought out the twist of paper I had wrapped it in. 'I came to bring you this.'

She tore it open and stared at the locket, her face tight with grief. 'There is blood on it.'

'Mine. I cut my finger on the clasp.' I held it up as proof.

She raised the locket slowly to her lips and closed her eyes, as if in silent prayer. A tear rolled down her cheek. 'Did he take it from her? How did you get it?'

'I found it on the ground.'

'Where?'

Again, I hesitated just a breath too long. 'In the street, outside the gate. She must have dropped it there.'

She shook her head.

'That cannot be true. I have searched the streets around the walls of your convent for the past two days for any sign of what happened to her. I would have seen it. And the chain is broken, as if it was torn from her.' When she saw that I was not going to respond, she rubbed at the tears with the back of her hand and drew herself upright. 'Well. I should not expect truth from a Dominican. But at least I know now that my sister is dead. She would never have willingly let this out of her sight.'

'Very wise. It is a beautiful piece of work. Your father must be a highly skilled craftsman, to have made something so complex.'

She looked at me with a hunted expression as she tried to discern my meaning. 'Did you open it?'

The question was barely a whisper. She knew the answer. She clenched her hands to stop them trembling and her face was tight with fear – the same fear I had felt only a moment before at her mention of Fontanelle. The naked terror of being found out.

'Yes. Is it your mother?'

She nodded, a tense little jerk of her head, her eyes still boring into me.

'She must have been beautiful,' I said. 'But something as valuable as that should be carefully guarded. Others might not be so understanding of your desire to honour your family memory.'

She gave a gulping sob and wrapped both hands over the locket. 'Thank you.' She swallowed. 'Did you show it to anyone? What is inside, I mean?' She glanced over her shoulder, as if I might have brought an army of Inquisitors to hide around the corner.

'No one but me. And I will say nothing.'

'Why?' That sharpness again; the muscles twitching in her jaw. 'Why should I trust you?'

'Because . . .' Because my own secret is far worse, I thought, and it is the very least I owe you for the fact that you will never truly know what happened to your sister. I could not say that. But the answer I gave her was also true. 'Because I believe God is bigger than the rules we impose on one another. I think He does not mind if we find different paths to Him.'

'That is heresy,' she whispered.

'So is that.' I nodded to the locket in her hand.

'You are a good man, Bruno,' she said. Unexpectedly, she leaned forward and placed a soft kiss on my cheek, at the edge of my mouth. She stood back and almost smiled. 'For a Dominican.' I could not look her in the eye.

'Wait,' she called, as I began to walk away. 'That man. The friar. Donato, is that his name? Where can he be found?'

'At San Domenico. Or at the Cerriglio, where you found him last night.'

'But he is always surrounded by people. I want to speak to him alone.'

'He would never allow it. Not after your last encounter.'

She shrugged. 'Still, I have to try. For my sister's sake. I just want to know.'

I considered this. 'He is rarely alone, except in his cell. Or perhaps when he takes one of the upstairs rooms at the tavern, to meet a woman.'

She nodded, tucking the information away. 'The cruellest part,' she said, with some difficulty, pausing to master her emotions, 'is that he has stolen from us even the chance to bury and mourn her properly. Whatever he has done with her, I can never forgive him for that.' I watched her teeth clench. She took a deep breath. 'Thank you,' she said, her voice harder this time, determined. 'For what you have done for my family. Perhaps we will meet again.'

'Perhaps.' I bowed and turned away. She would never know my part in what happened to her sister, but I would carry the weight of that knowledge with me always.

September rolled into October, apples ripened in the orchard and mists drifted in from the bay, though without a repeat of the previous year's fever epidemic. Fra Gennaro relaxed around me as he realised that I appeared to have suppressed my qualms and was not going to endanger him with a sudden eruption of conscience; he requested my assistance more frequently in the dispensary, and on occasion confided in me his notes and drawings from previous experiments, as if to demonstrate his trust. He promised to introduce me to a friend of his in the city, an aristocrat and a man of considerable influence as a patron of the sciences. As the weeks passed, I even managed to sleep through the night untroubled by dreams of the dead girl, though not every night.

But in other ways, my fortunes took a turn for the worse. It became clear that I had put myself on the wrong side of Donato, and that was a dangerous place to be. Perhaps he thought I knew too much, or perhaps he just wanted to remind me of his threat. I was summoned before the prior, charged with a series of minor infractions of the rules that he could not have known about unless someone was spying on me. I was given penance and a stern warning not to repeat the offences, as there would be no leniency in future. I lost the small freedoms taken for granted by the wealthier young friars, and found myself reduced to a life of prayer, worship and study – which was, I supposed, no more or less than the life I had signed up to in the first place, but it still chafed. The watch brothers were told to confirm that I was in my cell every night between Compline and Matins. My reading material and my correspondence were subject to unannounced inspections. Everywhere I felt his eyes on me – in the refectory, in chapel, in chapter meetings – and I could do nothing but watch and wait for him to strike. All this petty needling, I felt, was just a prelude. Donato was afraid of what he thought I knew, and he had something planned for me. The worst was not knowing what or when, so that I was permanently on my guard.

Over a month had passed since the night of the girl's death. The season was growing colder; at night, when we trooped reluctantly to Matins as the bells struck two, the air was tinged with woodsmoke and our breath plumed around our faces. I shuffled to my place in the chapel one night in October, stifling a yawn (there was a penance for that, if you did it too often), when I glanced across the choir and noticed the empty seats. Donato, Agostino, Paolo and at least two of the other younger friars had not returned in time for the service. This in itself was unusual; for all his swagger, Donato was careful to make an outward show of obedience. He reasoned that, as long as he was present at each appointed office, no one would question what he did in between. I could see that the prior, too, had noted the absences, though he made no mention of it.

Ten minutes into the service, I heard a disturbance at the back and turned to see Agostino rush in, his face blanched and stricken, the door clanging behind him. With no regard for propriety, he pushed through to Fra Gennaro and whispered in his ear; Gennaro immediately snatched up his candle and followed Agostino out of the chapel. The prior was furious at the interruption, his face slowly turning the colour of ripe grapes, but he mastered himself, exchanged a few words with the sub-prior, and disappeared after the troublemakers. The younger novices were almost bursting with excitement at the unknown drama and the sub-prior had to call us back to order several times. It was a small miracle that we managed to complete the office as if nothing was amiss.

Paolo was waiting for me in the cloister when I returned from Matins. I had never seen him look so shaken.

'Did you hear? Donato is dead.'

'What?' I stared at him. 'When?'

'An hour ago. At the Cerriglio.'

Heedless now of the watch brothers, I followed him to his cell and made him tell me everything.

Donato had taken a room upstairs at the tavern and engaged the services of one of the girls. After she left, he had called for hot water and towels to wash himself before returning to the convent. When the servant took the basin of water up to him there was no answer from the room. She knocked louder and then opened the door, to find him lying on the bed naked with his throat cut. You could have heard her screams at the top of Vesuvius, Paolo said. No one had noticed any disturbance from Donato's room earlier, though one of the other customers thought he had seen a new serving girl, one he did not recognise, loitering on the stairs by the back door shortly before the body was found. But Signora Rosaria had not hired any new serving girls recently, and this man was quite far gone in his cups, so his word was not worth much.

'They brought in the whore Donato was with, of course,' Paolo said, his voice still uncertain, 'though she swears blind he was alive and well when she left him a half-hour earlier. What's more, she didn't have a speck of blood on her, and you couldn't cut a man's throat like that without being drenched in it. I suppose that will not count for much, if they decide to accuse her.'

The strangest thing, he added, was that Donato's purse had been sitting there on top of his habit on a chair by the bed, in full view, and had not been touched. He shuddered. 'Think of it, Bruno. Naked and defenceless. Throat cut right across. It could have been any one of us.'

'Donato went out of his way to make enemies,' I said, carefully. 'I don't think you need to worry.'

'All the same,' he said, rubbing his neck with feeling, 'I think I might give the Cerriglio a miss for a while. Wouldn't hurt me to stay in and pray more often. I could learn from your example.'

'I would be glad of the company,' I said, forcing a smile.

The furore took a long time to die down. Fra Donato's father, Don Giacomo, was almost felled by grief; Naples had not seen such an extravagant and public display of mourning in decades. In return for hushing up the ignominious circumstances of Donato's death, the prior of San Domenico received a handsome donation, for which he was grateful, particularly since he knew it would be the last. Don Giacomo had intended his money to ensure his son's smooth ascent to election as prior one day; now there was no longer any purpose to his bequests. The whore Donato had been with before he died was arrested and quietly spirited away. Some days after the murder, they had found the bloodstained dress of a serving girl stuffed into a well a few streets from the inn, which was considered good enough evidence against the word of a whore. I never learned what became of her; I suppose she was hanged. No one else was ever found guilty of the crime.

The following spring, not long after the Feast of Candelora, as I was crossing Strada del Seggio di Nilo I saw a young woman moving towards me through the mass of people and for a moment my breath stopped in my throat. She carried a leather satchel across her body; a fall of glossy dark hair rippled around her shoulders, burnished in the sun, and she walked gracefully, with an air of self-possession. I withdrew into my hood and turned my face aside as she approached; I did not want to be recognised. If she saw me, she gave no sign of it, but as she passed, a splinter of sunlight caught the golden crucifix locket she wore around her neck, blinding me with a flash of brilliance. When I looked up again, she had vanished into the dust and crowds of Naples.

Find out more about S. J. Parris's bestselling Giordano Bruno series:

How S. J. Parris met Giordano Bruno

Acclaim for the series

More about the novels

On Giordano Bruno

I first met Giordano Bruno when I was a student and I
fell in love with him instantly. I was researching a paper
on Renaissance occultism when I came across a reference
to this intriguing Italian ex-monk, whose original and
unorthodox ideas seemed to get him into trouble wherever
he went, and immediately I set about digging up whatever
details I could find about him. What fascinated me most
about Bruno was the way he seemed to be a man with a
mind too modern for his time, an intellectual rebel, brave
enough to ask questions and pursue his theories about the
universe regardless of the consequences.

His life story often seemed like fiction — constantly on
the run from the Inquisition, fearing for his life, travelling
through Europe always in exile, dependent on courting
patronage from the powerful. Though we know quite a
bit about where he travelled and who he met, there is still
much about him that remains enigmatic, which is a gift
to a novelist. We know he must have been immensely
charismatic in person, since he went from living as a
fugitive to becoming personal tutor to the King of France
in only a few years. One of the few contemporary accounts
that survives of the real Bruno claims that everyone
wanted him as a guest at their dinner table for his lively and
controversial conversation. I knew from the beginning that
I wanted to put him in a novel one day.

Bruno came to London in 1583, at the age of 35, at the request of King Henri III of France. I had always been interested in Tudor England — Elizabeth's reign in particular was a time when the country was dangerously unsettled in its politics and religion (which were barely separate) and Elizabeth herself was the focus for a number of assassination plots by disgruntled Catholics. So when I came across the theory that Bruno — who was lodging with the French ambassador to Elizabeth's court — might have worked as a spy for Elizabeth's government, I knew I had found the key to telling his story in fiction with all the danger and excitement I had always felt it promised.

I found myself most interested in how Bruno would have fitted into this story; how he would justify to his own conscience the deceptions needed to be a successful undercover agent, how he would figure out where his loyalties lay. Like all spies and most fictional detective heroes, Bruno is essentially an outsider and has to weigh his own interests against the claims of loyalty and friendship. The Bruno who appears in my novels is, of course, my interpretation of the historical figure, taking those elements of his character that I found most compelling and reimagining him as a man who would have something to say to modern readers. I hope you enjoy his company as much as I have.

'Tense and lively, a welcome follow-up to *Heresy*, fully living up to its predecessor's promise'

Daily Mail

'Fascinating ...
The period is incredibly vivid and the story utterly gripping'

Conn Iggulden

'Hugely enjoyable'

Guardian

'The places and people are vividly described, and the solution to this exciting, well-written tale comes as a real surprise'

Literary Review

Heresy

**OXFORD, 1583.
A PLACE OF LEARNING.
AND MURDEROUS
SCHEMES.**

England is rife with plots to assassinate Queen Elizabeth
and return the country to the Catholic faith. Defending
the realm through his network of agents, the Queen's spymaster
Sir Francis Walsingham works tirelessly to hunt down all traitors.
His latest recruit is Giordano Bruno, a radical thinker fleeing the
Inquisition, who is sent undercover to Oxford to expose a Catholic
conspiracy. But he has his own secret mission at the University —
one that must remain hidden at all costs.

When a series of hideous murders ruptures close-knit college life,
Bruno is compelled to investigate. And what he finds makes it
brutally clear that the Tudor throne itself is at stake...

Prophecy

AUTUMN, 1583.
THE SKIES ABOVE
ENGLAND HARBOUR
DARK OMENS...

An astrological phenomenon heralds the dawn of a new age
and Queen Elizabeth's throne is in peril. As Mary Stuart's
supporters scheme to usurp the rightful monarch, a young maid
of honour is murdered, occult symbols carved into her flesh.
The Queen's spymaster, Francis Walsingham, calls on maverick
agent Giordano Bruno to infiltrate the plotters and secure
the evidence that will condemn them to death.

Bruno is cunning, but so are his enemies. His identity could
be exposed at any moment. The proof he seeks is within his grasp.
But the young woman's murder could point to an even
more sinister truth...